D0552128

My Daddy
is a
GIANT

For my little Else.
A kiss from your giant. ~ C.N.

First published in 2004 by Macmillan Children's Books
A division of Macmillan Publishers Ltd
20 New Wharf Road, London N1 9RR
Basingstoke and Oxford
Associated companies throughout the world
www.panmacmillan.com

ISBN 1 405 02167 5 HB
ISBN 1 405 02168 3 PB

Text copyright © 2004 Carl Norac
Illustrations copyright © 2004 Ingrid Godon

Moral rights asserted

All rights reserved. No part of this publication may be reproduced, stored in or
introduced into a retrieval system, or transmitted in any form, or by any means (electronic,
mechanical, photocopying, recording or otherwise) without the prior written permission of
the publisher. Any person who does any unauthorised act in relation to this publication
may be liable to criminal prosecution and civil claims for damages.

1 3 5 7 9 8 6 4 2 HB
3 5 7 9 8 6 4 2 PB

A CIP catalogue record for this book
is available from the British Library

Printed in Belgium by Proost

CARL NORAC

My Daddy is a GIANT

Illustrated by Ingrid Godon

MACMILLAN CHILDREN'S BOOKS

My daddy is a giant.
When I want to cuddle him,
I have to climb a ladder.

When we play hide-and-seek,
my daddy has to hide
behind a mountain.

And when the
clouds are tired,
they come and sleep
on my daddy's shoulders.

When my daddy sneezes,
it's like a hurricane.
It blows the sea away.

When my daddy laughs,

it's like another hurricane.

All the leaves fly off the trees.

Birds love my daddy.
They make their nests
in his hair.

When we play football,
my daddy always wins.

He can kick the ball as high as the moon.

But I always beat him at marbles.

His fingers are
far too big.

I like it when my daddy says,

"You're getting as tall as me!"

When my daddy runs,

the ground shakes

as if it was scared.

But I'm not scared
of anything when
I'm in my daddy's arms.

My daddy is a giant,
and he loves me with
all his giant heart.